SILENT
NATION

For Ian, who kept this book in shape

Titles in Teen Reads:

Fascination
DANIEL BLYTHE

I Spy
DANIEL BLYTHE

New Dawn
DANIEL BLYTHE

Underworld
SIMON CHESHIRE

Dawn of the Daves
TIM COLLINS

Joke Shop
TIM COLLINS

Mr Perfect
TIM COLLINS

Painkiller
TIM COLLINS

The Locals
TIM COLLINS

Troll
TIM COLLINS

Wasteland
TIM COLLINS

Copy Cat
TOMMY DONBAVAND

Dead Scared
TOMMY DONBAVAND

Just Bite
TOMMY DONBAVAND

Home
TOMMY DONBAVAND

Kidnap
TOMMY DONBAVAND

Raven
TOMMY DONBAVAND

Ward 13
TOMMY DONBAVAND

Fair Game
ALAN DURANT

Blank
ANN EVANS

By My Side
ANN EVANS

Living the Lie
ANN EVANS

Nightmare
ANN EVANS

Insectoids
ROGER HURN

Vanishing Point
CHERYL LANYON

Jigsaw Lady
TONY LEE

Mister Scratch
TONY LEE

Noticed
TONY LEE

Stalker
TONY LEE

Death Road
JON MAYHEW

Death Wheels
JON MAYHEW

The First Martian
IAIN MC LAUGHLIN

Snow White, Black Heart
JACQUELINE RAYNER

Silent Nation
BEVERLY SANFORD

Remember Rosie
BEVERLY SANFORD

The Wishing Doll
BEVERLY SANFORD

Billy Button
CAVAN SCOTT

Mama Barkfingers
CAVAN SCOTT

Pest Control
CAVAN SCOTT

The Changeling
CAVAN SCOTT

The Hunted
CAVAN SCOTT

Sitting Target
JOHN TOWNSEND

Deadly Mission
MARK WRIGHT

Ghost Bell
MARK WRIGHT

The Corridor
MARK WRIGHT

World Without Words
JONNY ZUCKER

Badger Publishing Limited, Oldmedow Road, Hardwick Industrial Estate, King's Lynn PE30 4JJ
Telephone: 01438 791037

www.badgerlearning.co.uk

SILENT NATION

BEVERLY SANFORD

Silent Nation ISBN 978-1-78464-609-7

Text © Beverly Sanford 2016
Complete work © Badger Publishing Limited 2016

All rights reserved. No part of this publication may be
reproduced, stored in any form or by any means mechanical,
electronic, recording or otherwise without the prior permission
of the publisher.

The right of Beverly Sanford to be identified as author of this Work has
been asserted by her in accordance with the Copyright, Designs and
Patents Act 1988.

Publisher: Susan Ross
Senior Editor: Danny Pearson
Editorial Coordinator: Claire Morgan
Copyeditor: Cambridge Publishing Management
Designer: Bigtop Design Ltd
© imageBROKER / Alamy Stock Photo

8 10 9 7

CHAPTER 1

RILEY

"...to make the most of your day!"

"Yeah, yeah, whatever." Riley poked her head out from under the bedcover and glared at the screen on the wall. "Stupid alarm!"

There was a rap on the door. "Riley? Are you up?"

Riley put her head under the cover and groaned.

The tapping got louder. "Riley! I'm not having you be late. You'll end up in the Assessor's office."

"OK, OK. I'm up." Riley sighed and swung her legs out of bed just as the news came on. As usual, the Newscaster was smiling brightly.

"Good morning, citizens! It's Thursday, it's 7am and the temperature is 23 degrees. You can expect dry, sunny weather all day and the current air quality warning is level 7. Now for the main news. A new Omega Valley Plant will open in Sector 10 today, marking a special moment for citizens who have been given roles there. 'It's a great opportunity for the lower-level Assessed,' the Third President said."

Riley frowned. 'The lower-level Assessed' were those who left school after Assessment, after being given roles at places like the Omega Valley Plants. Riley hoped she wouldn't be chosen for a role like that — she wanted to go to university.

"Are you out of that bed?" Mum wasn't giving up.

"You're as bad as that screen," Riley mumbled.

* * *

Mum put a bowl in front of Riley as she sat down at the kitchen table. Dad was glued to the breakfast broadcast, while Riley's brother Tommy watched cartoons on his tablet.

"Extra fuel for your exam," Mum said, as Riley dipped her spoon into the porridge.

"It's only history." Riley wasn't worried. She'd always found history easy — it was mostly old news films to watch.

"What's it about? I always liked history." Mum smiled.

"The Border Law," Riley said. "It's mad to see how people used to live."

"Yes, it was very different back then. Things were tough for our grandparents when were they little." Mum said.

"Great-Grandpa Henry lived in one room with his family, didn't he?" said Riley. "It must have been awful."

"They couldn't afford anything bigger," Dad said. Riley hadn't realised he was listening. "Henry's parents had lived in the First City all their lives; they didn't want to move. They had to rent one of those horrible boxes."

Riley had learned about the housing crisis in school. Some families had moved away from the First City while others crammed into tiny homes stacked up like boxes. "Why didn't the government help?" she said.

"That government? Fat chance!" Dad said. "They ruined the lives of hard-working people like my great-grandparents. All because of the Outsiders."

Riley knew about the Outsiders. Everyone did. They'd arrived on the island year after year, fleeing their own lands to escape disease and war. The island embraced them at first, but things began to change. After a while there wasn't enough to go around. Then crime began to rise — awful crimes that terrified the nation.

"Thank goodness for the First President," Riley's father said. "He was a proper leader. He saw the problem and he fixed it." He nodded firmly at the President on the screen. "And like his father and grandfather before him, this fella is made of the right stuff." He got up and left the room, muttering.

"Dad's still running the Presidential fan club, then?" Joni said, coming in. Riley hadn't seen her older sister since dinner last night. Joni was studying hard for her Assessment.

"You're running late," Mum said. "Eat quickly, you need to get to school. And don't be rude about your father." She stared at Joni until the teenager sat down.

"Well, honestly!" Joni said. "He's always on about how amazing the President is, how great the First President was, blah blah."

"That's enough," sniffed Mum. "Your father just appreciates how lucky we are. As should you."

Joni rolled her eyes as Mum walked out of the kitchen, dragging Tommy with her.

"It's like they're living in the past," Joni turned to Riley. "Why do we need to be reminded of that stuff all the time?"

Riley said nothing. She didn't know why Joni was so grumpy.

The Newscaster appeared on screen, smiling brightly. *"Good morning, citizens! It's Thursday, it's 8am and the temperature is 25 degrees. You can expect dry, sunny spells all day and the current air quality warning is level 7. Now for the main news. A new Omega Valley Plant will open in Sector 10 today, marking a special moment for citizens who have been given roles there. 'It's a great opportunity for the lower-level Assessed,' the Third President said."*

Joni slammed her spoon down. "Why do they have to work there?" she said.

"Because it's a great opportunity—" Riley began.

"No! It's because *he* says so." Joni jabbed her finger at the screen. "It's *his* system — he decides what we study, where we work, where we live... even our relationships have to be approved eventually!"

"So?" Riley said, putting her bowl in the dishwasher.

"You don't think there's anything wrong with the government planning your life for you?" Joni raised an eyebrow. "Seriously? You don't think you should have a choice?"

"I do have choices. And if you ask me, we're pretty lucky that the government helps us." Riley said.

"Really? OK, whatever you say." Joni got up and stomped towards the door. "I can see Dad's done a great job on you."

Mum walked in. "Girls! Why are you still here? You'll miss the TramShuttle!"

On screen, the bulletin was coming to an end with the regular message from Third President.

"Have a fulfilling Thursday and I hope you succeed in every way today."

"I'm sure you'll make him very proud, Riley," sniffed Joni, marching out of the kitchen.

CHAPTER 2

RULES

"I don't know what upset Joni," said Riley to her classmate Sonira, as they jogged around the school yard. "She's been so weird lately."

"Maybe she and Kyle had a fight," Sonira said. "Hey, isn't her Assessment coming up? She's probably worried about that."

"Yeah, maybe," Riley said. "She'll do fine, though. She's the brainy one." She stopped and leaned against the wall, catching her breath.

The smart band on Riley's wrist beeped loudly.

"Oh, what now?" Riley scowled, looking down. The band drove her mad sometimes. It was the law that citizens had to wear them, when they weren't sleeping or in the shower, and they were used for everything from sending messages and managing money credits to — in this case — keeping tabs on your exercise. The display flashed, noting that Riley had stopped jogging mid-lap.

The Instructor appeared on the screen nearest to her and spoke.

"Student 09OM-042, we have detected a change in your activity. Exercise is important for a healthy mind and body. Please continue with your exercise immediately unless you are unwell. If you are feeling unwell, please report to the Medical Unit."

Sonira jogged over. "Come on — only a few more laps to go!"

Riley sighed. "Don't those screens ever take a day off?" she said.

Sonira shrugged. "I don't really think about them. They're just kind of there, you know?"

Riley nodded. The Sector Wardens were always popping up on the screens. The Instructor, a dark-haired woman, helped students manage their school day. The Assessor, a grey-haired man, managed life stages like university and role. There were others, like the Juror and the Sector Guardians.

Riley wondered how you got a role like that — they were important ones. But for now, she had a zillion more laps of the yard to jog.

***

"Good afternoon, students. We hope you are ready for today's test. The test will last for sixty minutes. Please look at your screen to identify yourself and begin."

The Instructor smiled from the screen at the front of the learning centre. The big room was filled with students waiting to take their tests.

In a booth at the back, Riley put in her earbuds and looked at the screen. The robotic female voice of SAL — Student Automated Learning — spoke into her ears.

"SCANNING. PLEASE DO NOT BLINK."

Riley wanted to yawn. The eye scanners in Sector 9 were so slow. Her cousin Ruby lived in Sector 6, which had scanners that knew you on sight rather than scanning your eyes or thumb print. Just her luck that she lived in a sector that needed upgrades!

"IDENTITY CONFIRMED. HELLO, STUDENT 09OM-042."

Riley lifted her hand in greeting.

"YOUR TEST IS HISTORY LEVEL 5: THE BORDER LAW. PLEASE USE THE KEYPAD TO ENTER YOUR RESPONSES."

The keypad appeared on the surface below Riley's hands, the keys glowing softly in blue.

"QUESTION 1: WHAT IS THE BORDER LAW?"

Riley knew this one — it was easy! She typed: *The Border Law states that no person from outside the island is allowed to live on the island.*

Everyone learned about the Border Law in school. It was the most important law of all.

"QUESTION 2: WHAT EVENT IN 2022 LED TO THE CREATION OF THE BORDER LAW BY THE FIRST PRESIDENT?"

Riley typed: *The Centre for Governance was attacked by a group of men who stormed the building and killed staff members before setting fire to the building. They attempted to reach the First President but were overcome and captured before they could enter his office. They were part of an underground movement which planned to kill the First President and bring down the government. The men had moved to the island from Trelaya five years before. Other members of the group were found across the island after an investigation.*

Riley shuddered, thinking about how dangerous the island must have back then.

"QUESTION 3: IN 2030, WHY DID THE FIRST PRESIDENT PASS AN ADDITION TO THE BORDER LAW, BANNING CITIZENS FROM LEAVING THE ISLAND?"

Riley typed: *The First President banned citizens from leaving the island to prevent further outbreaks of the K-1FA virus, which had been wiped out on the island but was still active in other parts of the world. For the safety of all citizens, it…*

Fifty minutes later, Riley was done.

"WELL DONE, STUDENT 09OM-042, YOU HAVE COMPLETED THE TEST. YOUR RESULT IS: PASS."

All done! Riley breathed a sigh of relief. Another step towards her future.

CHAPTER 3

THE FIGHT

When Riley got home from after-school study, Mum was unloading the week's food supplies.

"I've got some new things," Mum said, showing Riley a jar of something brown and gloopy. "Look — this is that one they've been on about, Nutri-All. You only need a scoop to get your daily vitamins."

"It looks great, Mum," said Riley, screwing her nose up.

"I got some nice potatoes and leafy greens." Mum gave Riley a knowing look. "Greens are good for you."

Riley sighed. Greens turned up a lot at dinner. She had seen films of things people ate in the old days — some of it looked amazing. But with the borders closed, everything they ate now was grown or made on the island, mostly at the Omega Valley Plants.

The front door slammed. Seconds later, Joni came in, brown curls flying about her face. She ran a glass of water from the tap and gulped it down.

"Hey, Joni," Mum said. "Look what I got," she held up the jar of Nutri-All. "You're always complaining that we don't get enough vitamins."

Joni mumbled something under her breath.

Dad arrived home bang on time for the 6pm bulletin, as usual. As he stood in the kitchen, drinking a glass of milk, the Newscaster spoke.

"Good evening, citizens! It's Thursday, it's 6pm and…"

Riley was frowning over her nails when the breaking news caught her ears. She looked up as the screen showed an image of a Medical Unit spilling over with patients, many in makeshift beds, looking very ill.

"Reports are coming in about an outbreak of the K-1FA virus in the Federation of Misrovia. Alys Rey, Elected Leader, has declared a state of emergency. Medical Centres are filling up with the sick but medical teams are unable to get help to many affected areas because of blockades by rebel groups in protest against the Elected Leader. We now go live to the Centre for Governance to hear from the Third President."

Dad sighed. "Not again! They need to get some order over there."

The screen showed a white room with a silver desk, at which sat a broad-shouldered man with straw-coloured hair and brown eyes. Two masked Presidential Guardians stood behind him, guns in hand. The man looked into the camera, his face stern.

"Citizens, you will have seen the events unfolding in the Federation of Misrovia. I'm sure I'm not alone in wishing for help for the affected citizens and I hope they will find a way to control this latest outbreak. I would like to reassure you that you remain safe from this virus and from the rebel groups who seek to cause fear in the world. This, my citizens, is why we keep our borders closed."

Riley didn't take in what he said next as she was distracted by Mum putting bowls of food down. The family settled down to dinner.

"If they had a President like ours, they wouldn't be in this mess. They should have closed their borders," Dad rumbled, stabbing a potato with his fork.

"How?" Joni said. "They're not an island like us."

"There used to be checkpoints between the different nations," said Dad. "But then the war broke out and the virus, and you know the rest. Now it's just one disease-ridden, war-torn nightmare over there." Dad sniffed.

"How do you know what it's like?" Joni said. "You've never been there!"

"Joni!" warned Mum, 'Don't be rude. Honestly, I don't know what's got into you lately."

Dad looked up. "I see it every day on the news. I don't need to go there to know how terrible the rest of the world is."

Joni persisted. "But how *can* you know if you haven't seen it yourself? How do you know the government isn't just… *pretending* things are like that?" Her cheeks flushed.

Mum dropped her knife with a clatter.

Dad stared at Joni as if he'd never seen her before.

"What did you say?" he said quietly.

"I said, *how do you know?* You don't have any proof that it's true. None of us do! How can we if we've never seen it ourselves?" Joni's words tripped over themselves, trying to get out.

"Are you questioning the Third President?"

Joni stared at him defiantly. "I'm questioning his version of the truth."

"You're suggesting our President has lied to us?" Dad's voice was like ice.

"Yes — for a very, very long time."

"What exactly have we been lied to about?" Dad's face was going red, right up to his hairline.

"All of it. The viruses, the wars, about people from other nations being dangerous."

"Outsiders," Dad stood up and faced off against his daughter. "They are called *Outsiders*, Joni."

"Aren't we outsiders too — in other nations? They didn't close their borders to us, did they? What about all those citizens who were stranded because the First President wouldn't let them come home? He wasn't acting in the best interests of the people then, was he?" Joni was fuming.

Dad put his hand to his head. "Where has all this come from?" he said slowly, as though in pain. "Why are you saying these things?"

"Because it's the truth!" Joni spat out. "We've been lied to over and over by your precious President. Keeping the people under control like one of those awful rulers from history! He's evil, the same as his father and grandfather before him. You're just too stupid to see it!"

"GO TO YOUR ROOM!" Dad bellowed at her.

Riley had never heard Dad raise his voice before.

Joni threw back her chair, sending it crashing to the floor. "Liars ruling fools," she said viciously as she stormed off.

The front door slammed.

Mum burst into tears.

CHAPTER 4

JONI

When Joni hadn't come home by 10pm, Riley was worried. She'd messaged her sister three times but had no reply. The young adult curfew was 10pm and if Joni was caught out by the Sector Guardians, she'd be in big trouble. It would affect her next Assessment score and the family could receive points on their Community Licence, which led to heaps of problems. Some families even moved away to lower grade sectors when that happened.

Riley had never forgotten her friend Felix, who lived two homes along when she was small. She and Joni often played with him. He made up brilliant stories and adventures, and he could build clever things, like tiny robots. Joni always said he would grow up to be the Head of Technology at the Centre for Governance.

But Felix changed. He grew terrified of the screens, claiming that they could 'hear' and 'see' things. He tried to hide from them at first, then got angry and tried to shut them down when they came on for the bulletins. After it happened a few times, Mum said he wasn't well and that the Medical Advisors should 'fix him'. She tried to stop the girls from playing with him but they sneaked out when she wasn't looking.

One bright day in the summer, Felix attacked the screen in his bedroom with a hammer. Riley could hear him yelling all the way from the garden. Mum said a neighbour must have called the Sector Guardians, as they arrived in minutes.

"They'll take him to the Medical Centre," Mum said, arms around the girls. "He'll get help there. But my goodness, this will affect their Licence."

Felix never came back home. The family moved away a few weeks later and when Riley asked Mum if she could contact him, Mum said she needed to forget about him. The next week, a new family moved into Felix's house, with twin girls who never yelled when the news bulletins came on. Riley tried to play with them but they wouldn't go on adventures and they didn't like building anything.

Riley thought of Felix as she stood at her window in her pyjamas, watching for Joni. She didn't know what to do. Dad had gone to his club, still furious. Mum had gone to bed with a headache. Riley wanted to go to bed, but she knew she wouldn't sleep while Joni was still out.

Suddenly, she saw a shadow in the front garden — Joni! She crept downstairs and opened the door but Joni wasn't there. Riley sneaked outside, squinting in the darkness, but she couldn't see Joni. She was about to go back in when she heard a sound coming from the middle of the garden where a large tree grew. As she got nearer, it got louder — someone was crying. Looking up, she saw a shadow in one of the lowest branches.

"Joni?" she whispered. "Are you up there?" The snuffling stopped abruptly.

"Go inside," Joni whispered. "I don't need Dad coming out and shouting again."

"He's at the club. Come down, it's past curfew."

"I'm in our garden — that's not against the law. Now go inside."

Instead, Riley pulled herself up on to the thick branch where Joni sat, tucked against the trunk, arms clasped around her knees.

"What are you doing up here?" Riley said.

"Remember how we used to sit up here?" Joni whispered. "We thought nobody could see us."

Riley did remember. She and Joni hid up there when they were younger, giggling among the leaves. Joni's favourite game was to pretend they were somewhere else.

"You used to say we were in Misrovia," Riley said. "With those funny striped creatures that jump about."

"Yes," said Joni. "You know, they're so tame that you can ride them."

"*Could.* It's sad that they're all gone now."

"Says who? The President?" Joni said, sarcasm cutting through the dark.

"They're extinct. You know that!"

"Do I?" Joni suddenly tapped Riley's arm. "Where's your band?"

"Indoors. I was waiting to go to bed." Riley said. "Why?"

Joni huddled deeper into the tree. "Nothing, don't worry." She paused. "What happened after

I left?" she asked. "Did they say anything?"

Riley hesitated. Dad had said quite a few things but she didn't want to upset her sister.

"Just tell me."

"Dad said you sounded like one of those rebels. You know, the ones they caught last month."

Joni laughed bitterly. "Dear old Dad. He'll never change. He won't see those people as anything other than bad."

Riley didn't know what to say. It had been big news, the discovery of a rebel group in Sector 15 who didn't agree with how the island was governed. The news said the group had planned to kill the Third President. They were found guilty of treason. "Prison's too good for them," Dad had sniffed at the screen. "They would have got the death penalty once upon a time!"

Joni had shaken her head at that and left the room.

"I expect he'll never forgive me, either," she continued, pulling at the leaves. "But I wonder what he'll do about it."

"What do you mean?"

"His own daughter speaking out against the President? I bet he's told his club buddies already."

"He'd never do that!" Riley was shocked that Joni would even think that. "It was just a fight. It'll be OK in the morning."

Joni sighed. "It won't." She looked at Riley. "Remember that story you liked, about the man who found out his life was an illusion?"

"Yeah," said Riley. She loved that story. A man learned that his whole life was a false reality created and controlled by machines. He had to choose whether to stay in the false world or live in the dangerous real world.

"Well," said Joni, "imagine that it's like that, right here, right now."

Riley nearly laughed out loud. "Yeah, OK, we're ruled by machines. That'd be so cool!"

"Would it?" said Joni. "Remember Felix?"

Riley tensed. "Of course I do. He was so ill."

"Was he? What if he was right?" Joni dropped her voice lower. "What if the screens really are spying on us?"

"Don't be silly. Why would they want to see inside our homes?"

"Not just our homes, Riley. They're everywhere — or have you never noticed?"

They *were* everywhere, Riley thought. At school, on the streets, on the TramShuttles.

"Ever tried turning one off during a bulletin?" Joni asked. "It doesn't matter if you haven't, because even if you tried, you couldn't."

Riley remembered Felix going crazy whenever a bulletin came on. She'd never understood why they bothered him so much. They'd always been there, as long as she could remember. The screens were like part of the family — they greeted you, they woke you up, they gave you reminders and information. Mum always said she didn't know what she'd do without them.

"They're always on," she suddenly realised.

"Sssh!" Joni warned, "Keep it down. But yes, exactly. Turning themselves on, talking to us by name — quite the member of the family, aren't they?" She sighed. "Like a hotline to the government, 24/7. And don't get me started on these." She tapped her smart band.

"But why would anyone be watching us?" Riley said.

Joni smiled. "The government wouldn't want us turning into rebels, would they? Or finding out about their lies."

"You keep saying that. What lies?"

"Maybe they do want us to be safe, who knows? But I think if you lie to people for long enough, they'll believe it. If you can keep scaring people, say by claiming a virus is still raging in the rest of the world, people will believe it."

"That doesn't make any sense. Why would they do that?"

"Maybe to keep people under control, so they won't question anything." Joni said. "And the worst lie of all? The Outsiders."

"No way were they a lie," Riley shook her head.

"I'm not saying they weren't here. But they lied about the Outsiders being a threat and they *definitely* lied about what happened to them."

"They went back to their own nations. I've seen the films at school."

"All of them? They went away, just like that, huh?"

"OK, then. What do you think happened to them?"

Joni leaned in and whispered in her ear. "I think they're still here."

CHAPTER 5

MISSING

Riley blinked. Still here? Now she really did think her sister had lost her mind.

"But where?" she stammered. "We would have seen them. You can't hide that many people."

"Can't you?" Joni said. "Powerful people can do anything they like. Look, there's something really important we need to—"

She was interrupted by a TramShuttle stopping at the end of their street. "Goodnight, Mr Thorn and thank you for travelling," said the robotic voice of the Automated Passenger Assistant.

"Dad!" whispered Joni. "Quick!" She started clambering down the tree. Riley followed. The girls only just made it back inside their bedrooms before Dad walked in the front door.

Riley waited under her bedcover as Dad went into the bathroom and then the bedroom. It wasn't long before he was snoring loudly. She tiptoed to Joni's room and without knocking, went inside.

Joni was sitting on the floor, fiddling with her tablet. Riley sat down opposite her, cross-legged.

"You should be in bed," Joni said, as if the entire night hadn't happened.

"We need to talk about something?" Riley said.

Joni widened her eyes and darted them to the side.

"Huh?" said Riley.

Joni made a tiny gesture, pointing towards the screen on the wall. Riley looked and saw a tiny white light flashing in one corner of it. She'd never noticed it before.

"Are you still worrying about your exam result?" Joni said, her voice sleepy but her eyes alert. "I told you before, you'll be fine."

Riley played along, still not sure why she was supporting this crazy idea of Joni's. "Yeah. I guess I'm just being silly."

"It's not silly. But let's talk about it tomorrow?" Joni's eyes were wide. "It's late, you should get some sleep."

"OK," said Riley.

"Let's do something after school tomorrow. We haven't done that for ages. Sorry, it's my fault. I've been so busy. We'll talk about it all tomorrow, OK?" She stood and extended a hand to Riley, pulling her into a hug. "Don't say anything," she whispered in Riley's ear. "I love you. You know that, right?"

"I love you too," Riley whispered, hugging her sister tightly.

* * *

Joni wasn't there the next morning. It wasn't unusual as she often went for a run before school. Mum wasn't happy about it, though. "She should have made an effort after last night," she said, putting the porridge down. "She owes your father an apology."

"Mmmm," said Riley, hoping Mum would drop the conversation.

"When you see her at school, you can tell her I expect her to come straight home afterwards. We need to have a talk," Mum continued. "This silly behaviour has got to stop. It'll ruin her chances of getting a good role. And goodness only knows if anyone heard her. What will the neighbours think?"

Riley didn't care what the neighbours thought.

There was a stuffy old couple on one side and a family on the other who acted like they were from Sector 2 or something. She was more interested in hearing the really important thing that Joni needed to tell her.

***

Riley didn't see Joni all day and Joni didn't reply to her messages. Riley waited at the gate after school, but as the students slowed to a trickle, she wondered if Joni had forgotten. She decided to go home.

"Hey, Riley? Wait a second!"

Turning, she saw Kyle, Joni's boyfriend, coming over. She didn't know him very well, although he and Joni had been together for ages. They kept to themselves, which annoyed Mum. "He's distracting you from your study," she complained to Joni whenever she had a chance. But Joni was smitten with the brainy boy from her Tech class.

"Hey," Riley said to Kyle. "Do you know where Joni is?"

Kyle frowned. "I was about to ask you the same thing. She didn't come to school."

"Are you sure? She was gone before I left this morning." Riley felt tugs of worry in her gut.

"She didn't sign in and she hasn't replied to my messages." Kyle bit his lip.

"Or mine," said Riley.

"Did she say anything about going anywhere today?"

"No," Riley said. "All she said last night was that she'd meet me after school."

Before Kyle could reply, one of the street screens came on. *"Good afternoon, citizens! It's Friday, it's 5pm and…"*

Kyle glanced at it. "Let's walk," he said.

* * *

Kyle kept his voice low as they walked, looking around him as if he expected someone to jump out.

"She came to see me after the fight. She wanted to stay but I made her go home because of the curfew. How was she when she got in?" he asked, his face troubled.

"She said a lot of crazy stuff," Riley said.

"Like what?"

"The stuff she said to Dad… about the government, about them lying to us. And… this was the craziest bit — she said the Outsiders were still *here*." Riley hadn't realised she was talking loudly until a woman ahead of them turned around and looked at her.

Kyle stopped and grabbed her arm so tightly that his knuckles went white. "Did anyone hear her?" he whispered urgently.

"Ow!" Riley wrenched her arm away. "No, we were quiet. I don't know why she said that stuff, anyway." She rubbed her arm, rattling the band on her wrist as she did so.

Kyle looked at it, then at Riley, his eyes widening. He shook his head and put his finger to his lips.

"What?" Riley was convinced that everyone was going crazy.

Suddenly, the band beeped. Kyle backed away, horror all over his face.

"It's Mum," Riley said, reading the message on it. "I need to go home."

"Is Joni there?" Kyle said.

"I don't know."

"Can you ask her to message me?" Kyle was desperate. "I need to know she's OK."

"Yeah, OK," Riley turned away, "Sorry. I have to go." She jogged towards an approaching TramShuttle, leaving Kyle standing in the street.

* * *

As Riley reached home, she saw a Sector Guardian transport parked outside. "Oh great," she said. "That's all we need!"

The door opened as she walked up the path. Mum stood in the doorway, eye make-up and tears making muddy tracks down her face.

"Mum? What is it" Riley rushed towards her. Mum looked *awful*.

"Where have you been? It's your sister. She's gone, Riley. Joni's dead!"

CHAPTER 6

SECRETS

"A tragic accident," they called it on the scrolling news bulletin.

Riley stared at her bedroom screen. 'A tragic accident' didn't even begin to cover it. Not the giant hole in her heart, not the aching pain in her body, not the questions raging around her head.

Riley had sat numbly while a Sector Guardian told her how Joni's body had been found at the bottom of an old quarry on the outskirts of their sector, near where she went running. He said a strip of her trousers was found on a branch near the top; she must have tripped and tumbled down the rocks to the floor below. "The impact to her head would have killed her instantly," he said, sending Mum into fresh sobs.

"She was lying there all day," Mum had wailed. "My little girl, all alone like that." She put her head in her hands while Dad sat stiffly beside her, his lips pinched.

Riley had gone to her room then, frozen with shock. Unable to sleep, she stared at nothing as the bulletins came and went.

* * *

Joni's memorial was a few days later. The family gathered with a small group of neighbours and classmates in their sector's memorial room while a Counsellor on the screen ran through Joni's life like a list of bullet points.

Riley didn't like memorials, they were cold and strange. Her lessons had taught her that in the old days, citizens sang songs and recited things called prayers at memorials. Many believed their loved ones would go on to another life after death — Riley liked that idea.

As the family left the building, Riley noticed that two Sector Guardians were standing outside.

"Why are they here?" she said but Mum wasn't listening. She was trying to comfort Tommy, who was shaking with tears. Riley didn't know why Dad had made him go to the memorial. He was too young to understand it all.

Someone touched her elbow. "Ignore them," Kyle said quietly, beside her. "They just like to keep an eye on everything, don't they?"

"How are you doing?" Riley asked. He looked like he hadn't slept for days.

"Sad. Angry. You know?" Riley's heart went out to him. He looked as destroyed as she felt. "I don't know what to do without her."

Riley nodded. "Yep." Pausing, she realised she should reach out to him. "Look, Kyle, you can message me anytime if you need to. I know it's hard."

Kyle looked around before speaking. "That's really kind, Riley. I know we don't really know each other, but Joni talked about you so often."

Riley felt comforted by that. She sometimes thought Joni found having a little sister annoying.

"Actually, there is something you can do, if you really don't mind?" Kyle's eyes darkened.

"Sure. What is it?"

"I gave Joni a teddy bear, an old fashioned one."

Riley smiled. Joni might have been tough as old boots sometimes but she was a sucker for a teddy bear. She refused to get rid of the ones she'd had when she was little.

"I know the one." Kyle had got Joni a special bear for her last birthday. It was an original bear from many years ago. She loved it.

"I'd like to have it. Do you reckon your parents would mind?"

Riley didn't think so. "I'll see what I can do," she said.

Kyle smiled tightly. "You've no idea how much that means to me," he said. "Thank you."

* * *

Riley looked everywhere for the bear but she couldn't find it. Kyle was upset when she messaged to tell him.

"It's got to be there somewhere. Sorry, I know I'm being a pain, but you have to find it."

"I'll keep looking," she wrote back, but she didn't know where it could have got to.

That night, she stood in the front garden and looked up at the stars for a while. It was too intense indoors. Mum and Dad were wandering about like zombies and Tommy was hiding in his room. She needed a bit of space.

She had a few flowers in her hand. She and Joni used to leave surprises for each other in a secret place in their tree. Flowers, stones, sweets — gifts to make each other smile. Riley thought she'd leave some pink flowers there for Joni.

Climbing up, she felt around for the place. Suddenly her hand touched something soft. The bear! "What are you doing here?" she said to it. The bear stared back, keeping secrets.

She hugged it and bent over her band, about to message Kyle with the good news. But as she pressed the bear to her body, she felt something move under its soft red jumper.

She pulled out a strange metal device from under it. It was small and thin, with a display screen and some buttons. She pressed them but nothing happened. She'd never seen anything like it before.

Riley wondered if it was a project that Joni had been working on in Tech but if so, why hide it? What did it do? And was *this* what Kyle had been so desperate for her to find?

***

The next day, at lunchtime, Riley marched into the Senior Tech room, looking for Kyle. A few students were dotted around the benches, working on projects and computers.

She spotted him, head bent over a tablet, deep in conversation with a curly-haired boy. "We need to talk," she said, standing over him.

The two boys nearly jumped out of their skins.

"Woah! Don't sneak up on people like that!" Kyle yelped. "What are you doing here?" he said in a low voice.

"We need to talk," Riley repeated, arms folded.

"You shouldn't be in here. It's for Senior Tech students," Kyle frowned.

Riley stared at him. "I don't think anyone will tell me off for talking to my dead sister's boyfriend, do you?"

The curly-haired boy looked up. "She's got a point."

Kyle scowled at him. "Shut up, Louis. You *know* she shouldn't be in here." The boys exchanged a look.

Riley was getting annoyed. Something was clearly going on.

"We need to talk about *this*," she said, pulling the bear out of her bag.

Kyle reacted as if he'd been burned. "Hell, Riley! Put that away right now." He quickly pushed the bear into her bag. "You shouldn't have brought that here."

"You asked me to find it," Riley said through gritted teeth.

"Yes, OK, I did, and thank you. I'm very grateful that you have. Just not here, OK?" Kyle pleaded with her.

"Then where?" Riley said. Now she *knew* something was going on. This was way bigger than some boy just being embarrassed about a teddy bear in front of his mate.

"Tomorrow before breakfast, at the secret garden," Kyle whispered quietly in her ear.

Riley froze, her head spinning with emotion. "Where?" she said, faintly.

Kyle looked into her eyes. "You heard."

Kyle had invaded Riley's memories without warning. The secret garden was the name she and Joni had for an old nature area they loved exploring when they were little. It was overgrown now and people hardly ever went there.

"See you there?" Kyle said, shepherding Riley towards the door.

"Yep," Riley just about managed, still stunned.

"Good. One more thing. The bear — he's all there, isn't he?" Kyle stared at her intensely.

Riley jolted to attention. So, it *was* the device he was looking for.

"He sure is," she said.

The weight dropped from his shoulders instantly.

"Thank you," he said. "Thank you very, very much."

CHAPTER 7

SURPRISES

Perched on a tree stump at the edge of the nature area, Riley sat huddled against the early morning chill as she watched the path for Kyle.

"Hey." Kyle was behind her. She didn't know where he'd come from — all there was in that direction was thick woodland. There weren't even any screens around here now, the place was deserted.

"You came," he smiled.

"I said I would."

"Cool," Kyle said. He had the same intense look on his face that he'd had the day before.

"Are you on your own?" he asked, looking around.

"Yes."

There was an awkward pause then Kyle spoke. "Did you bring it?"

Riley put her hand on the bear, tucked inside her bag.

"Yes."

Kyle raised an eyebrow. "So… can I have it?"

Riley shook her head. "Not until you tell me what's going on."

Kyle sighed. "I don't have time for this."

"Tell me what that thing is and I'll give it to you."

Kyle stared hard at her.

"What?" Riley said.

"I'm thinking."

"About *what*?" Riley had no idea how Joni had put up with this boy. He was infuriating.

Kyle suddenly snatched Riley's bag from her shoulder and pulled out the bear, quickly patting its jumper.

"Hey!" said Riley, but then without warning he pulled out the device, grabbed her wrist and held the device over her smart band. The band lit up and the display flashed before settling back down. "There you go," Kyle said, handing Riley her bag.

"What did you do?" she said, looking at her band. "Is it broken?"

Kyle smiled. "Not exactly. I've just stopped them from listening in. For now, anyway."

"Who's 'them'?" Riley was wary. "Who's listening?" First Joni and now Kyle too?

"The Guardians, the government — all of them. We have to be careful."

Riley backed up. "I didn't come here to get dragged into all that stuff again!"

"Didn't you? I thought you wanted to know the truth. That is why you're here, right? Otherwise you would have just handed that bear straight over."

"The truth about what?"

"Do you believe that what happened to your sister was an accident?" Kyle looked so serious that Riley's heart thumped. "Think about it."

Riley's mind whirled as she thought of her sister. Joni, who went running for miles. Joni, who had never even sprained an ankle. Joni, who had been behaving so very oddly. Shutting her eyes, she whispered, "No."

When she opened them again, Kyle had tears in his eyes. "No. And neither do we."

"Who's we?" Riley looked around.

"You'll see. If you want to, that is?"

"I don't know what I want. I just wish Joni was here." Riley brushed tears from her cheeks furiously.

"I know. And so do I," Kyle said.

Riley swallowed. She didn't know what she was getting herself into. But the thought of Joni lying dead at the bottom of the quarry was too painful to ignore.

"Yes," she said through her tears. "I want to know the truth."

Kyle smiled and jiggled the bear in the direction of the woods. "Good. Then we're going this way."

* * *

"Ow!" Another branch scratched Riley as they trekked through the dense woodland. They hadn't seen another person in the hour they'd been walking.

"Nearly there," said Kyle.

"You still haven't told me where 'there' is," said Riley.

Minutes later, Kyle walked under a sweeping canopy of dull green leaves. Riley followed and gasped in surprise — almost completely hidden by the leaves was the front of an old building, paint peeled down to the walls.

"You've dragged me all this way to go to some old… whatever *this* is?" Riley said.

Kyle tapped four times on the rusty door. After a moment, it swung open, revealing a boy with kind blue eyes and a shock of dark hair.

Riley clapped her hand to her mouth.

"Hello, Riley," Felix said. "It's been a long time, hasn't it?"

CHAPTER 8

TRUTH AND LIES

Riley's head was still spinning as Felix secured the locks behind them inside the building. "I hoped Kyle would persuade you to come here," he said.

"I don't understand — how are you even here?" Riley looked from him to Kyle, confused. "You two know each other?"

Felix smiled. The small, jumpy boy from Riley's childhood was now a tall, slim teenager with a quiet calm about him. "Yes, we do. Sorry for the shock. You've had enough of those lately." He touched her on the arm. "I'm so sorry about Joni."

Riley bit her lip. "Thanks," she managed.

Felix looked at Kyle. "Have you got it?"

Kyle nodded. "Yeah, she brought it, safe and sound."

Felix sighed in relief. "Good. Thanks, Riley. You have no idea how worried we were. We didn't know if Joni had it on her when she — well, you know." He looked uncomfortable.

Riley drew her breath in sharply, realisation hitting her. "You knew Joni too? I mean, since you moved away?"

Felix gestured forward, "Yes. Come on, I'll explain. Watch your step, the floor's a bit dodgy."

The story unravelled as they walked further into the dark building, Felix lighting the way with a torch.

"My Aunt Julia still lives in this sector — do you remember her?" Felix said. "She's ill, so I pop in and make sure she's OK when I can. Nobody seems to blink an eye at me visiting. I'm a well behaved citizen these days."

Kyle laughed. Riley wasn't sure what the joke was.

Felix continued. "I bumped into Joni as I was waiting for a TramShuttle to go home one day. She recognised me straight away. We chatted for ages and she said something that I'll never forget. She said, 'I always believed you, Felix.'" He looked sad.

"How long ago?" Riley asked.

"Last year."

"What? Why didn't she tell me?" Riley was starting to feel like she hadn't known her sister at all.

"She needed to protect you."

"From what?"

"You'll see. No more secrets now." Felix touched her on the shoulder. "I promise."

"Why didn't you come and see us if you were here?"

"I didn't think you'd want to see the crazy kid," Felix said. "I bet your mum wouldn't have been pleased to see me, either."

Riley couldn't help but laugh, "No, probably not. I guess you're not scared of the screens anymore, though."

"As it turns out, I shouldn't have been scared of them," Felix said. "I should have been scared of the people behind them."

"You sound like Joni," Riley said.

"Yes," Felix said, simply.

Just then, they reached another doorway.

"This whole place used to be a renewable energy station, so we figured it was OK to repurpose it," said Kyle. "Welcome to our base."

"Base?" Riley raised an eyebrow.

"Haven't you worked it out yet?" Kyle said. He tapped on the door four times. "We're rebels, Riley."

* * *

"So all this time, Joni was here with you?" Riley's head was spinning.

"Sure was," Kyle said. "Well, she did go running sometimes. But mostly she was here."

"Did you get her into this?" Riley said.

"Joni? Hell no." Kyle smiled. "It was her who persuaded *me* to join these crazy pirates."

Riley had been introduced to some of the rebels after entering the inner rooms. They looked just like normal teenagers working on their projects in a Tech group. "Except with some dangerous ideas," Kyle said when Riley told him.

"We found each other through our Tech groups," Felix explained. "There are others too, across the island, but everyone here is from nearby sectors. Well, apart from me. I haven't found anyone else in mine yet."

"Are you like those rebels on the news?" Riley wondered.

"No, they weren't part of our network. In fact, they probably weren't rebels at all." Felix looked serious. He tapped Riley's band. "Now, we don't want you off the radar for too long, they might notice. Let's get cracking."

"How *did* you do that, anyway?" Riley asked Kyle.

Kyle chuckled. "If we couldn't find a few little tricks to get around the government's spying eyes, we wouldn't be top of the class, would we?"

"Hey, Riley! Welcome to the party." The curly-haired boy from Kyle's Tech group walked over.

"You too?" Riley shook her head. She couldn't believe what was happening.

"I'm Louis, by the way." He waved a strange kind of helmet at Felix and Kyle. "Guys, I've got it going again. It was just the wiring."

"Perfect timing," Felix said, taking it from him. "Riley's popped over for a history lesson."

"What is this?" Riley touched the strange device.

"They were really popular once. They could show people scenes that felt totally real — another planet, another land — whatever they wanted. Like living in a film. But people loved their fantasy worlds more than real life, so these got banned." Felix held it out. "And with some tweaking, they can also give you a history lesson. Go ahead, put it on."

Riley put the helmet on her head. It covered her ears and eyes.

Kyle spoke. "This might be a bit freaky but just remember we're right here."

"We're rolling!" Riley heard Louis call.

Suddenly, she was looking straight at a woman's face. Sounds hit her all at once — crying, wailing, people talking in a strange language. She was surrounded by a crowd of people of all ages, carrying bags and cases, children clutched close. Uniformed men with guns stood nearby. She knew this scene — she'd seen it in history lessons. This was a processing point for Outsiders, before they left the island. "They're going home," Riley said. "They look really scared."

The scene changed abruptly. It was night and the Outsiders were huddling through tall metal gates, while guards watched over them. Riley looked around. "Where are we?" she asked. Her question was soon answered.

As her view moved through the gates with the Outsiders, she saw it. A symbol she saw every day in her kitchen — a wheat spike with writing over it: Omega Valley Plant.

"What are we doing here?" she said. The scene changed again. Now she was in a dimly-lit room crammed with bunks. A group of female Outsiders stood together as a pale thin man addressed them.

"Welcome to your new home. You are the lucky ones. Here there is no war, no virus. You have been allowed to remain here. But you must earn your keep."

Riley gasped out loud.

The scene changed, blurring through different faces, young to old. Now she was in a huge indoor room, where Outsiders dressed in dirty blue overalls were hard at work, operating big machines as sweat poured from their heads. They were mixing brown and white liquid and churning it along huge pipes. Riley noticed that nobody looked at anyone else, nobody smiled. Everyone just worked.

The scene moved on, this time showing female Outsiders working in an indoor garden, tending to rows upon rows of plants. Some pulled vegetables from the ground, wiping dirt from their faces with filthy headscarves. Riley winced — the false sunlight in the room was too bright. Sweat trickled down her brow — she was sure she could feel the heat from the plant room.

A woman working on potato plants suddenly called out as she fell on to the soil, clutching her tummy. A mean-faced man in a uniform marched over and without warning, kicked her in the back. "No!" shouted Riley, but they couldn't hear her.

"It's not the end of your shift!" he shouted. "Get back to work!" But the woman kept crying out. Another woman ran over. "Please," she begged him. "She's with child!" The guard cursed and spoke into his wristband. "This is Overseer 9177. I need a new one up here on potatoes." He grabbed the woman and pulled her roughly away from the ground. "Get off the soil, you're damaging the product."

Riley felt sick to her stomach. "I've seen enough!" she whispered.

The factory disappeared immediately and the helmet was taken off. Kyle's face swam into view. "Are you all right?" he asked. She nodded.

He handed her a cup of something warm and sweet-smelling. "Drink this, it'll help. It's hard the first time you see it. But you needed to."

Riley looked up at him. "Was that real?"

He nodded. "Every bit. We spliced it together from old sources. Some from security cameras, some filmed by those workers before their tablets were taken away."

"But how come we've never seen it?" Riley said. "Surely something that shocking would get out?"

"Our guess is that anyone who tried to leak anything just disappeared." Felix said. "But the government certainly kept the footage — there's loads of it. We finally managed to hack their systems a while back and we've been stealing stuff like those films from right under their noses."

"And they've never caught you?" Riley was amazed.

"So far, no. They're over confident, which is their weakness. But we've also got the best nerds around." Felix smiled.

Riley had to know something else. "Joni said the Outsiders were still here. But that stuff I just saw — that was from the old days, wasn't it?"

Felix looked grave. "Just so you know, Riley, we don't call them Outsiders here — they're people." He paused. "And the pregnant woman from the film? She had her baby last month. She named him Eli."

CHAPTER 9

REBELS

Generation after generation, born into slavery. Riley couldn't even begin to process it.

"So the films I've seen of people leaving were lies?" she said.

"Not all of them," said Felix. "Many did leave. But then somebody high up had an idea. You see, the rest of the world didn't think much of us sending people away. And we had to produce a lot more food as we couldn't get it from outside the island anymore. It was the perfect solution."

"A life of slavery or a life of war and illness," Riley said, shaking her head.

"Many didn't want to go home anyway, so some probably went to the factories willingly, believing they would have a good life. But they were lied to." Felix frowned.

"But the lower-level Assessed work at those places," Riley said. "Surely they told people about it?"

"If you knew you would pay the ultimate price for blabbing, what would you do?" Felix raised an eyebrow.

"I'd tell everyone," Riley said. "They've no right to make people into slaves — it's wrong!"

Felix smiled. "Now who sounds just like Joni?"

"It's not only islanders who work at the plants," Kyle spoke up. "Many of the overseers are from worker families, born inside."

"They've turned on their own people?" Riley was shocked.

"They do what they have to. They're born into slavery, into awful conditions. They're just trying to survive," Kyle said.

"How did you find all this out?" Riley said. "It's not like you can walk into the plants and ask to look around."

"Joni," said Kyle proudly. "She worked out how to tap into the security screens."

"You can hack the screens?" Riley was amazed.

"Yeah, you're just hitching a ride on their tech, seeing through their eyes. They can't even tell you're doing it." Kyle said. "Joni had been working on it for ages. She was determined to crack their sneaky spying eyes."

"And they found out," Riley suddenly realised.

"About her hacking the plants? No." Kyle shook his head. "But we're pretty sure she was on a watch list. The screen activity in your home was huge. Somebody out there *really* wanted to know what she was up to."

"But they did kill her?"

"We can't prove it," Kyle said. "But they've wiped all the footage from the screens near where she was found. We couldn't find anything and trust me, we looked."

"But if they didn't know she was hacking them…" Riley didn't understand.

"She forgot the rules, Riley." Kyle's eyes were fierce. "The outbursts with your dad, the conversations with you — it lit her up like a beacon. They probably silenced her as a warning."

Riley swallowed hard.

"She was going to leave," Kyle blurted. "If we'd gone sooner…" His face crumpled.

"What?" Riley was stunned. "She was about to do her Assessment — she wasn't going away."

"We're all leaving," Felix said. "It was the plan before Joni died and we're still going through with it. We're going to free the workers."

"You're going to *what?*" Riley nearly fell off the chair.

"We're going to free them," Felix said calmly. "We'll take them away from the island and once we're in Misrovia, every islander will see a very special news bulletin — one that shows what's really been going on."

"Are you crazy?" Riley wondered if her mother had been right about Felix after all. "Apart from anything else, it's dangerous over there. There was an outbreak of the virus and—" She stopped. Felix and Kyle were smiling at her. "Why are you looking at me like that?"

"There wasn't an outbreak last week," Felix said gently. "It's totally under control. And the war was over some time ago."

"Why would they lie about that?" Riley didn't believe it.

"If you thought it was safe there now, you might want to go there," Kyle said. "And then you might think the border should be opened in full again."

Riley realised what he meant.

"Trust me, it's perfectly safe — we've made contact over there," he continued. "The communication is a little rusty, but we're getting there."

It was all too much for Riley to take in. "So how," she said, "do you plan to leave the island with a group of escaped workers without anybody noticing?"

Felix winked. "We've got a brilliant plan."

* * *

As Riley walked through the woodlands with Kyle, her mind spilled over, churning with everything she had just learned. The plan was insane.

"There's a big tunnel under the sea," Felix had said, showing Riley a blueprint. "Trains used to run through it all the way to Misrovia. They shut it when they closed the borders."

"Please tell me you're not planning to steal a train?" Riley said.

"Ha!" laughed Felix. "We've never tried that. No, we're going to casually walk through the tunnel to the other end. It's not as far as you might think."

"But you said it's closed," Riley said.

"We've found the door code," Felix said. He exchanged a look with Kyle. "Look Riley, we're leaving tomorrow night. We're really doing it. And you can come too, if you want to?"

Riley didn't know what to say then and she still didn't know.

"You don't have to decide now," Kyle said as they went back through the woods. "Think about it and message me later. Just be careful what you write. We can't give them any sniff of our plans."

"Was she really going to do it?" Riley couldn't believe her sister would have gone through with it.

"All the Sector Guardians on the island couldn't have stopped her," Kyle said. "But there's something you should know. If you do this, we might never come back."

"I might never see my family again?"

Kyle shook his head.

"Will they be at risk?" Riley had to know.

"They'd be questioned and then monitored probably forever, but they'd be OK. They're not involved."

At the tree stump, Kyle hugged her. "There isn't a right or wrong choice," he said. "She'd understand whatever you decide." He zapped her smart band and walked away without looking back.

CHAPTER 10

CHOICES

Mum and Dad were too numb to pay attention to Riley's claim that she'd gone for an early morning walk. Usually Dad would have joked that the only thing that got Riley doing exercise was the promise of a treat at the end, but this time he barely noticed that she'd spoken.

Alone in her room, she tried to make sense of it all. The fact that Joni had been planning to leave her family was too painful to think about.

Missing her sister's closeness, Riley went into Joni's room. It was just as she had left it. Mess everywhere, clothes all over the floor. Mum hadn't been able to face cleaning it up.

Riley felt the pain well up as she looked around — everything was just so Joni. Her nature pictures on the wall, her beloved 'proper books', the tiny teddy she'd had since forever and refused to get rid of. Riley picked it up and hugged it.

She lay on Joni's bed, breathing in the memories. Could she do it? What about Tommy? What about Mum? Losing one daughter was bad enough, but two? She buried her head under the pillow and cried silently until there was nothing left to come out.

"Ugh," she sniffed, rubbing her sore eyes. Sitting up, she looked for a tissue but couldn't see any. She leaned over the edge of the bed and poked around under it, not finding anything. Suddenly, she knocked something into view — a notebook.

"What's this?" Riley wondered. She was about to pull it out when the screen behind her on the wall clicked on for the bulletin.

Riley's heart beat fast. Thinking quickly, she pulled a shirt across the floor and over the notebook. "I was looking for that shirt," she said loudly. Folding the shirt around the notebook, she got up and casually walked out of the room.

＊＊＊

Tucked out of sight in the tree, Riley opened the notebook and flicked through. It was mostly poems and stories. Smiling at Joni's messy handwriting, Riley was about to close the notebook when she noticed a turned corner on a page near the back. It was a letter.

Dear Riley,

If you're reading this, I'm already gone. I don't want you to be sad, even though I know you will be. If everything has gone to plan, by the time you find this, I'll be in Misrovia.

All those things I've been trying to tell you — they're true. I'm going to prove that to everyone — even Dad! They lied to us about so many things, Riley, and I have to make sure they can't do it any longer.

Please don't hate me for leaving. Remember that I'll always be your sister. Maybe we'll see each other again one day if things turn out OK.

Look after them for me.

I love you.

Joni xxx

Fresh tears spilled down Riley's cheeks. Joni must have planned to leave the letter for her.

"I don't know what to do, Joni," she whispered to the setting sun.

* * *

"…and tonight's news. A new Omega Valley Plant will open in Sector 23 next month. 'It will truly benefit citizens,' said the Third President."

"Good," said Dad, chewing his potato mash. "They'll be able to grow a lot more food with another factory."

Riley put her fork down. She couldn't eat her potato now that she knew what had gone into growing it. In fact, she didn't think she could ever eat an Omega Valley Plant meal again.

"Are you OK?" Mum said, "You're very pale."

"I've got a headache." Riley lied. "Sorry, Mum, I don't think I can finish this." She pushed her plate away.

Mum felt Riley's forehead. "You're a bit warm. Maybe you should get an early night." She looked anxious.

"Yeah, I will," Riley said, feeling guilty for making her worry.

She hugged Mum extra tight, kissed Dad and gave Tommy a big squeeze. In her room, she tapped on her smart band. She'd made her decision.

"Yes." She sent it and waited.

Moments later, he replied. "I'm glad."

CHAPTER 11

DANGER!

Riley hadn't seen the man at first. She'd been wandering along trying to look like she was just out for a stroll and not like someone who was about to go on a stupidly dangerous mission. Her mind was full of home — Mum and Dad had gone out with Tommy; she'd waved them off with a smile. She was fighting hard against the instinct to run right back home to them.

As she turned a corner, she heard footsteps and looked behind her. A hooded figure was catching up to her fast! She walked faster but so did the footsteps. Breaking into a run, she pelted across the street. The figure followed, so she ran into a side street and then into an alley. The footsteps had stopped. Aching with the effort of trying to outrun the stranger, she hid behind a large bin, trying to catch her breath. After a minute she peered out — the stranger was nowhere in sight. Breathing a sigh of relief, she adjusted her bag and stepped out.

A hand gripped her arm. "Don't make a scene," a deep male voice warned.

Riley twisted, trying to free herself, but his grip was too strong. "Get off me!" she cried, as a cuff was fastened around her wrist. She hit out with her other arm, catching the man's hood, which fell back to reveal a mean-looking older man.

"Don't try that again!" he warned, gripping her un-cuffed arm. "Your sister made that mistake with me, and she ended up at the bottom of a quarry."

Riley swore and spat in the man's face. "Murderer! Know what they do to men like you?

The man sneered. "For killing a traitor? They gave me a reward for that. Now, we're going to have a nice talk," he said. "You're going to tell me all of your sister's secrets. If you're a good girl and tell me the truth, I might even let you go."

At that moment, two Sector Guardians ran into the alley. One pointed at Riley and the pair walked over to where she and the man stood. "That's it," Riley thought. "They've found out!"

"Well done. We'll take over from here," one said to the man.

"Hang on, they weren't my orders," the man said.

"We've received information about a rebel cell. We're taking her in. Do you want to discuss it?" The Guardian put a hand on his baton.

"I'm not handing her over without my payment," the man grumbled. "I caught her."

"Fine," the other Guardian snapped, her voice slicing through her helmet. "Come with us and collect it from the Juror's Centre."

The trio marched Riley along the alley and into the back of a transport. She sat quaking in fear as they drove away. What would happen to her now? Had they got the others?

"Where are we going?" said Riley's captor a moment later. "The Juror's Centre isn't this way."

"We've had word that another rebel is nearby," the male Guardian said.

"Kyle!" thought Riley. They'd arranged to meet. She had no way to warn him!

The vehicle pulled into another alley and Riley saw Kyle up ahead. She tried to yell out but the man put his hand over her mouth.

"Shut up!" he snarled as Kyle turned and saw them. He stood still as they pulled up and the male Guardian got out.

"You're late," Kyle said in a low voice, grinning.

"We had trouble catching her. She went for a run." The Guardian pushed his visor up to reveal twinkly eyes behind it — Louis! Riley thought she might faint with relief.

"What the—?" the man said as the other Guardian touched him on the head with a silver stick. He slumped in the seat. The Guardian zapped the man's smart band with a device that Riley recognised.

"What a charmer," said Vix, a rebel with red hair and a huge grin, lifting her visor and winking at Riley.

"We spotted him hanging around when we checked a feed near your home," Kyle said, climbing in the back as Louis got in the operator's seat. "Luckily, we had a plan B."

Riley smiled. "Nice ride too."

"She's great," said Louis, reversing back down the alley. "Can you believe this poor darling was waiting to be scrapped? She just needed a bit of love. We've had her for a while. She's very handy."

"What about him?" Vix asked, looking at the man slumped next to Riley.

"Cuff him and dump him in the woods," said Kyle.

"He killed Joni," Riley said. "He admitted it."

Kyle's expression darkened. "Maybe we'll lock him in that bunker we found. He'll never find his way out."

CHAPTER 12

THE PLANT

Riley didn't find out what they did with the man who murdered Joni. Kyle and Louis took him away, still unconscious, while Riley waited with the group at a meeting point. Nobody asked them about it when they returned. "Best not to," Vix whispered.

As the transport left their sector, Felix went through the details, making sure everybody knew the plan.

Riley didn't know how they were going to pull this off. It seemed far too easy. The plant, which she'd seen on the film at base, was in Sector 31.

"It's one of the oldest Omega Valley Plants and it's not as well guarded as others," Felix said. "It's on the coast, so it doesn't get much attention." Few people lived around the coast now, instead choosing to live in urban sectors with more roles and modern homes.

"There are guards here and here," Kyle said, pointing at the map. "Not many though. There's not much risk."

"Risk of what?" Riley asked.

"Workers escaping," Kyle said.

"How do you know that?" Riley asked.

"We got lucky when we hacked this plant," Felix said. "The guards don't shut up; they give away all kinds of useful information. And then there's our inside man."

"You've got a contact in there? How?" Riley was amazed.

"We broke in. We did a bit of sneaky tech and made a few friends. It was our most dangerous mission until now. David, our contact, is an overseer, born inside. He wants out, along with many of his people. He's been very helpful."

"Do you trust him?"

"Completely. Joni did too. She was the one who found him," Felix said.

Riley shook her head. What else would she find out about her sister? "I just hope she was right."

* * *

Hours later, Riley peered through the bushes, waiting as Kyle tapped on his tablet. The screen outside the Plant's main gates flickered briefly.

"That'll keep it quiet," he said. "If anyone checks the feed it'll show the same nice, quiet view it's had all evening."

There was a movement to the left of the gates. Vix appeared out of the bushes and gave a thumbs up.

"Let's go," Kyle said. The group slipped though the dark and over to the gate.

"Both of the guards are down," said Vix. "They'll be sleeping in the bushes for the rest of the night." She held up a smart band. "I borrowed this from one of them too. Makes things even easier." She touched the band on the gate panel and it swung open.

Riley's skin prickled. Kyle saw her unease. "They can't see us," he said. "I promise." It didn't make Riley feel any better.

It was dark and silent inside the gates. Sneaking around the edge of the yard, the rebels headed towards the factory buildings. Every so often Kyle fiddled with his tablet, checking that their presence was going unnoticed.

"Why aren't there guards here?" Riley wondered.

"Like I said, they don't need them," said Felix. "The workers aren't allowed out here, so there's no risk of escape. Ah — here we are."

They had reached the back of a big building. Felix looked at the door. "Any minute now," he whispered.

The door opened silently and a man in an overseer's uniform stepped out. He smiled, "My friends, you came."

* * *

"Riley, this is David," said Felix. "David, this is Joni's sister, Riley."

David bowed his head, then took Riley's hand. "I'm sorry for your loss," he said kindly. "I liked Joni very much."

"Thank you," said Riley, touched.

"Are we good to go?" Felix asked.

"Some of my fellow workers are enjoying an extra-long sleep," David smiled. "But those of us who are coming are ready."

He led them away from the building and over to a battered doorway. Riley could barely make it out, it was so small.

"It's not pretty down here," Felix warned her as they stepped inside. "This is where everyone lives." They descended down a steep flight of steps, with David using a candle to light the way.

The Outsiders' sector was even worse than Riley had seen on the film — it was like a giant cellar. It stank of a hundred years of sweat and misery, and rats scuttled everywhere. The group slipped quietly past dingy rooms filled with bunks, many with sleepers in them, while peeling metal pipes and dirty furniture made the corridors feel even smaller. Riley gulped in snatches of grim air. "It's a prison," she thought.

As they walked, Riley learned that many Outsiders hadn't wanted to leave — they feared it too much. But others did and they were waiting up ahead. "Aren't you worried they'll tell?" she whispered to David.

"We choose carefully down here," he said. "Some families can be trusted, some can't. I've been here long enough to know who I can trust." He patted the badge on his uniform.

"You really are an overseer?" she whispered.

David smiled grimly. "Yes. There are quite a few of us. We're useful. It means the guards don't poke around down here too often." He winked. "And sometimes it means better rations for my friends."

"Haven't you ever tried to escape before?" Riley couldn't help but ask.

"Why would we? We were born here, we're prisoners here. We didn't know there was another choice until your friends found us."

He patted her on the arm. "Until we met your sister."

Riley couldn't even begin to imagine the life David had led. Falling silent, she followed him along the corridor.

Soon they saw a light in the distance. As it grew closer, shadows moved around the walls. Riley realised that people were sitting there. The light moved and she saw old and young faces. In the dim glow, she could see their eyes were full of hope.

The Outsiders.

CHAPTER 13

ESCAPE

Riley felt like she couldn't climb another stair. They were roughly built and she kept stumbling. They'd walked for ages, creeping through dirtier, older tunnels that seemed to be less man-made and more like caverns.

"We're under the back of the factory land now," Felix said ahead of her. "Nobody knows where these stairs came from but they go back to the old days at least."

"Why didn't we just go back out the way we came in?" said Riley.

"Too risky," said Felix. "It'd only take one guard to arrive or an overseer to blow the whistle and the whole thing would be over. We couldn't risk any of the workers waking up and seeing the others sneaking out either — like David said, they choose their friends carefully here."

A whisper from above meant that Kyle and David had reached the top. A sliver of moonlight shone down as Kyle paused to use his tablet to deal with any screens, although Felix had assured Riley that only one small screen was on the back gate. "There's nothing out here," he said. "They don't even have a guard most of the time. Nobody ever comes to the coast anymore, do they? People are still scared that they'll catch the virus from the ocean."

The group climbed out of the steep opening as David ushered his friends towards a high fence. Despite the dark, Riley could see a narrow gate in it. Louis crept over to it and fiddled until it swung open.

"There's always a back door," winked Kyle. "And we're always good at finding it."

Suddenly there was a shout from behind them — a man in an overseer's uniform was climbing out of the opening behind them!

"What the hell…? Who's he?" Vix hissed. "David, shut him up — quickly!"

"Abraham," David met the man half way across the ground. "Old friend — have you decided to join us after all?"

The man shook his head angrily and began talking in another language. David answered him. Riley didn't know what they were saying but it was clear they didn't agree.

"Won't they be listening in on his band?" she realised in a panic.

"They don't have them. They're not citizens," Felix said, looking worried as the man's tone grew more agitated. He whispered loudly. "David, what's—"

Suddenly Abraham hit out at David. David tried to defend himself, but Abraham was stronger. "He's going to turn us in," hissed David to his friends. "You must go!"

Vix didn't wait. She ran towards the pair and there was a struggle as she pushed herself in between them, shoving David aside. Vix raised her silver stick and Abraham fell to the ground, pulling her with him. He didn't move.

"Vix?" whispered Felix. "Vix?"

"I'm OK," she whispered back. "I got him."

What happened next was so fast that Riley could never quite remember it after. As Vix tried to get up, a knife flashed through the moonlight, into her back.

"No you don't!" Vix groaned, grabbing Abraham as he tried to get away. She held the silver stick against his chest and he moaned, then fell to the ground.

"Go!" Vix called to her friends, a dark patch spreading across her shirt in the moonlight. She gave a thumbs up, then collapsed, dead.

CHAPTER 14

THE TUNNEL

Riley loved the salty air of the sea — it was new and amazing.

"The smell of freedom," David said next to her. "My grandfather travelled for many weeks to reach this island, in search of freedom."

"Why did he come?" asked Riley.

"It was safer than where he came from," David said.

Riley's chest tightened as she thought of her own family – would they be safe after this? And Mum

– oh, Mum! She must be so worried by now. Sobs swelled up in Riley's throat.

"We're nearly there." David said. "Take strength from that." He squeezed her hand.

It had been a long, tiring walk through the night along the old coastal paths, but he was right. They were nearly there.

* * *

The tunnel entrance was almost invisible from the road.

"You really wouldn't have a clue that the North tunnel was through there," said Kyle. Now covered in plants, it was a haven for wildlife.

"They don't want anyone to know it's there," said Felix to Riley, tucking the blueprints into his pocket. "There are no working screens here either. That way it looks like there's nothing to protect."

Riley wasn't so sure. "It doesn't feel right," she said.

"Don't get jittery." Felix said.

"We've checked this place out," Kyle said. "It's dead. There's a gateway code to get into the tunnel itself, as you know, but we've got that."

"Why does it need a code if the tunnel is shut?" Riley said.

"It's just old," said Kyle. "They put it on there when the border closed."

"Doesn't anyone ever try to come through from the other side?" Riley wondered.

"They know the island is closed off; it's hardly a welcome party!"

"Let's get moving. It's nearly dawn," called Felix.

* * *

"It isn't working." Kyle was frustrated. "I've tried it three times."

"That doesn't make sense," Felix said. "Are you sure you got the code right?"

The pair went inside to join Louis, who was still trying.

Riley, along with the others, was crammed against the overgrown weeds and tendrils, trying to stay out of sight.

Moments later, there was a shout from inside the tunnel entrance. The boys ran out, Kyle yelling, "Move! Move! She's going to blow!"

Riley and the others just had time to get back before there was a sound like rumbling thunder and a huge cloud of dust tumbled out of the door. The entrance collapsed into rubble in front of them.

CHAPTER 15

FREEDOM

"It was rigged to go off after a certain number of tries," Louis said, brushing dust out of his curls. "A retro booby trap!"

"Probably with a retro hotline to our favourite people," Kyle said. "We need to get out of here before they turn up. I *knew* we should have just hacked it instead of using that old code. I said so before, didn't I? Felix — what do we do now?"

Felix was looking at the rubble in silence. Riley stood by in shock, while David tried to calm the upset Outsiders.

"Felix?" Kyle repeated.

Riley walked up to him. "What's plan B, Felix?" she said quietly.

"We don't have one," Felix said faintly.

"There *has* to be," whispered Riley, looking at the Outsiders. "They can't go back. We have to do *something*. Here, give me that." She snatched the rolled up blueprint from his pocket and stared at it, looking desperately for answers. Suddenly, something caught her eye.

"Felix, there's another tunnel. The South tunnel."

Felix shook his head. "We already looked at it but we can't use it. There was a train accident before it closed and they blocked it off — see?" He pointed to a greyed out section at the Misrovia end of the tunnel.

But Riley had seen something else. "Yes, but there's *another* tunnel between the North and South — a utility tunnel. If we can get into the

South tunnel, we can go along the utility tunnel back into the North one."

"Riley's right!" Kyle said, peering over her shoulder. "I don't know why we didn't think of it before but we can totally do that."

"You were probably too excited about the hacking to spot the obvious," Riley gave a wry smile. "So can we hack the door properly this time?"

Felix smiled. "Yes, we can hack the door properly this time." He grinned at her. "You're bloody brilliant, Riley. Let's do it!"

The South tunnel was exactly the same as the North, overgrown and hidden. Riley stood outside, fingers in her ears as the boys hacked the door.

"We're in!" called Louis from inside. Riley beamed at David.

The group was soon walking through the dirty old South tunnel, under the sea. It was eerie and dark, with echoes of the past floating around it — old papers, rusty tin cans, even old shoes. Rats scuttled and spiders crawled along the walls. It must have been beautiful once, Riley thought, looking at the smooth walls and train tracks.

"Another hour and I reckon we'll join up with the utility tunnel," Louis said. "By the time our nice government friends work out where we are, we'll be half way to Misrovia."

"What if they catch up with us?" Riley whispered to Kyle. "They're bound to have traced that explosion by now."

"I reset the door code, remember? They'd have to hack it themselves to get through. And if they do, we'll put up a fight."

"They're better armed than we are, we won't last long," Riley watched as a woman ahead stopped and leaned against the wall. "Look at them — they're exhausted," Riley continued, "What hope do they have if we're caught? We can't let it happen, Kyle. They've come too far to get caught now." Her eyes shone with tears. "Joni wouldn't want that."

Kyle nodded, his own eyes wet. "Then I guess it's up to us, isn't it?"

Riley smiled. "Yes, it is." She went over to Felix, who was walking with David. She pulled him to one side. "Felix, we have to go back," she whispered.

"What? Why?" Felix was horrified.

"Not all of us." Riley looked over at Kyle. "Just me and Kyle. Felix, you know they'll get through that door behind us. Everyone's exhausted — we have to make sure they make it. For Joni."

Felix looked at Riley with furious respect. "She'd be so proud of you," he said.

Riley nodded. "I hope so. Now, we're going to need anything you've got."

***

When the Alpha Unit arrived at the South tunnel entrance, the door inside was firmly locked.

"Hack it," said the Unit Commander. "They could have gone through and reset it. They wouldn't have just given up at the North entrance. The President wants this rebel cell caught and shut down today. And trust me, none of us want to let him down."

His squad started work, leaving a lone guard standing outside with their transport. As he waited, he heard a slight noise behind him and turned around. "Morning!" smiled Kyle, as he knocked the guard out with one of Vix's favourite devices and the man slid to the ground. Kyle ran across the road, away from the tunnel, and hid in the undergrowth.

"This is for freedom!" yelled Riley beside him as she pressed the detonator linked to the explosives they had placed in the tunnel entrance.

"Boom!" she whispered.

Two months later

"It's working — I can see your face this time!" Riley said with excitement as Felix swam into view. "Look Kyle, we can see him!"

Felix waved at them through the screen.

"How's Misrovia?" Riley asked.

"The weather's nice," said Felix. "But we've got a lot of work to do. How's the new HQ?"

"It's not bad," said Riley, looking around at the old wartime bunker. "It's not Sector 1 level comfort, but we can't complain. Their silly old trackers can't reach us in here."

"Speaking of which," said Felix, "How's our film project coming along?"

Riley smiled. "It's coming along just fine. We've nearly finished splicing it together. We just need a bit more time — they've got a bit tighter on security recently. Anyone would think they were worried about something!"

Felix chuckled. "Well, if anyone can do it, you two can."

"It'll be a bulletin to go down in history," Riley said, beaming at the screen. "Good morning, citizens! Breaking news: it's time to show you the truth…"

THE END

ABOUT THE AUTHOR

Beverly Sanford is from East London. She currently works in social media and in motorsport, and previously worked in TV, music and theatre before becoming a writer. She has written two other Teen Reads for Badger, *The Wishing Doll* and *Remember Rosie*, as well as two non-fiction titles, *Social Superstars* and *Amazing Racing — the world of Formula 1*. When not writing, Bev is probably watching Formula One or West Ham United, listening to music or eating cake.

Author photo: Photo © Jan Dunning